Angel Child, Dragon Child

ISBN 0-590-42271-5
Text copyright © 1983 by Carnival Press, Inc.
Illustrations copyright © 1983 by Vo-Dinh Mai.
All rights reserved. Published by Scholastic Inc.,
730 Broadway, New York, NY 10003, by arrangement with
Raintree Publishers, Inc.

12 11 10 9 8   1 2 3 4/9

Printed in the U.S.A.   08

First Scholastic printing, August 1989

ANGEL CHILD, DRAGON CHILD

story by MICHELE MARIA SURAT
pictures by VO-DINH MAI

Scholastic Inc.
New York Toronto London Auckland Sydney

My sisters skipped through the stone gate two by two. Mother was not there to skip with me. Mother was far away in Vietnam. She could not say, "Ut, my little one, be an Angel Child. Be happy in your new American school."

I hugged the wall and peeked around the corner.

A boy with fire-colored hair pointed his finger. "Pajamas!" he shouted. "They wore white pajamas to school!" The American children tilted back their long noses, laughing.

I turned away. "I want to go home to Father and Little Quang," I said.

Chi Hai's hands curved over my shoulders. "Children stay where parents place them, Ut. We stay."

Somewhere, a loud bell jangled. I lost my sisters in a swirl of rushing children. "Pa-jaa-mas!" they teased.

Little Quang (kwang)   *Chi Hai (chee hi)*

Inside, the children did not sit together and chant as I was taught. Instead, they waved their hands and said their lessons one by one. I hid my hands, but the teacher called my name. "Nguyen Hoa."

Hoa is my true name, but I am Ut. Ut is my at-home name—a tender name for smallest daughter.

Nguyen Hoa (new-yen hwa)

"Hoa," the teacher said slowly. "Write your name, please." She pressed a chalk-piece to my hand and wrote in the air.

"I not understand," I whispered. The round-eyed children twittered. The red-haired boy poked my back.

"Stand up, Pajamas!"

I stood and bowed. "*Chao buoi sang*," I said like an Angel Child. The children screeched like bluejays.

chao buoi sang (chow bwee sung)

I sat down and flipped up my desk top, hiding my angry Dragon face.

Deep in my pocket, I felt Mother's gift—a small wooden matchbox with silvery edges. I took it out and traced the *hoa-phuong* on the lid. When I tapped the tiny drawer, Mother's eyes peeked over the edge.

"I will keep you safe in here, Mother," I told her. "See? You will just fit beside the crayons."

hoa-phuong (hwa fung)

Her listening face smiled. In my heart, I heard the music of her voice. "Do not be angry, my smallest daughter," she said. "Be my brave little Dragon."

So all day I was brave, even when the children whispered behind their hands and the clock needles ticked slowly. Finally, the bell trilled. Time for home!

As soon as he saw me, Little Quang crowed, "Ut! Ut! Ut!" His laughing eyes gleamed like watermelon seeds. I dropped my books and slung him on my hip.

There he rode, tugging my hair as I sorted mint leaves and chives. Little Quang strung rice noodles from the cup hooks. Father and I laughed at this happy play.

At night, small brother curled tight beside me. I
showed him Mother's lonely face inside the
matchbox. Together we prayed, "Keep Mother safe.
Send her to us soon." With Mother's picture near, we
slept like Angel Children.

In this way, many days passed.

One day at school, small feathers floated past the frosty windows. "Mother," I whispered, "this is snow. It makes everything soft, even the angry trees with no leaves to make them pretty."

My fingers danced on the desk top while I waited for the bell. When it rang, I rushed out the door.

Outside, snowflakes left wet kisses on my cheeks.
"Chi Hai!" I called. "Catch some!"
"It disappears!" she cried.

Just as Chi Hai spoke, a snowrock stung her chin.
That red-haired boy darted behind the dumpster. He
was laughing hard.

I tried, but I could not be a noble Dragon. Before I
knew it, I was scooping up snow. My hands burned
and my fingers turned red. I threw my snowrock and
the laughing stopped.

Suddenly, the boy tackled me! We rolled in the snow, kicking and yelling, until the principal's large hand pinched my shoulder.

"Inside!" he thundered, and he marched us to our classroom.

We can't have this fighting. You two have to help each other," ordered the principal. He pointed at me. "Hoa, you need to speak to Raymond. Use our words. Tell him about Vietnam." Raymond glared. "And you, Raymond, you must learn to listen. You will write Hoa's story."

"But I can't understand her funny words," Raymond whined. "Anyway, I don't have a pencil."

"Use this one, then," said the principal. He slapped down a pencil, turned and slammed the door. His shoes squeegeed down the hall.

Pajamas!" Raymond hissed. He crinkled his paper and snapped the pencil in two. He hid his head in his arms. How could I tell my story to *him*?

The clock needles blurred before my eyes. No! I *would not* be an Angel Child for this cruel-hearted boy.

But later, across the room, I heard a sniffle. Raymond's shoulders jiggled like Little Quang's when he cried for Mother.

I crept over. Gently, I tugged the sad boy's sleeve. He didn't move. "Raymond," I pleaded, "not cry. I give you cookie."

Suddenly, his head bounced up. "Hoa!" he shouted. "You said my name. You didn't use funny words." He broke off a piece of the cookie.

"I say English," I answered proudly. "And you call me Ut. Ut is my at-home name, from Vietnam."

"Okay, *Ut*," he mumbled. "But only if you tell me what's in your matchbox."

"My mother," I told him. We giggled and ate the cookie crumbs.

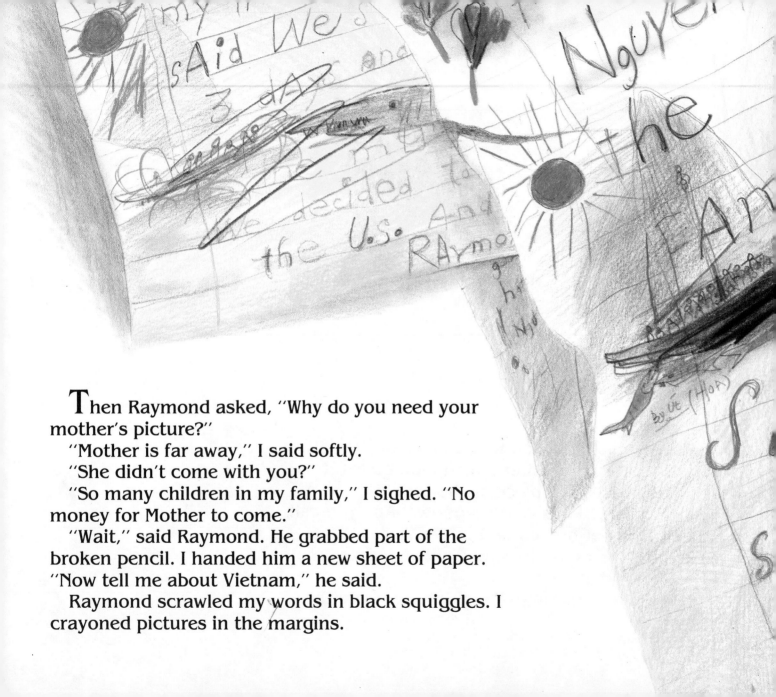

Then Raymond asked, "Why do you need your mother's picture?"

"Mother is far away," I said softly.

"She didn't come with you?"

"So many children in my family," I sighed. "No money for Mother to come."

"Wait," said Raymond. He grabbed part of the broken pencil. I handed him a new sheet of paper. "Now tell me about Vietnam," he said.

Raymond scrawled my words in black squiggles. I crayoned pictures in the margins.

When we were ready, Raymond leaned out the door. "Done!" he beamed. He waved the story like a flag.

The principal squeegeed up the hall. "You may go," said the big man.

We dashed through the stone gate together.

The next day, the principal read our story to the whole school. "These girls sailed many oceans to be here. They left behind their home, their friends, and most important of all, their mother. So now. . . ."

"Ut's mother needs money for the long boat ride to America!" shouted a familiar voice. Raymond stood on his chair. "And we could have a fair and *earn* the money."

"Young man!" warned the principal.

Raymond slid down in his seat. "We could," he insisted. I hid my eyes. I held my breath. Chi Hai squeezed my hand.

A special fair! A Vietnamese fair!" my teacher exclaimed. My eyes opened wide.

The principal's eyebrows wiggled like caterpillars. "But who will help with a Vietnamese fair?"

"Me!" cried Raymond.

"We will!" squealed the children.

"Well, what are we waiting for?" said the principal. And we all clapped for the fair.

On the special day, I wore my white *ao dai*
and welcomed everyone to our Vietnamese fair.
"Chao buoi sang," I said, bowing like an Angel Child.
"Chao buoi sang," they answered, smiling.

ao dai (ow zi)

High above our heads, our rainbow dragon floated freely. Below, Chi Hai and her friends sold rice cakes, imperial rolls and sesame cookies. Raymond popped balloons and won three goldfish. He gave one to Little Quang. "Don't eat it," he warned.

By the end of the day, we had just enough money to send to Mother. "When will she come?" I wondered.

Every day, we walked home wondering, "When will Mother come?"
We slid through icy winter. . . .

We splish-splashed through spring rain. . . .

We tiptoed barefoot through the grass, still hoping she would come.

On the last day of school, when I knew the
hoa-phuong were blossoming in Vietnam, Raymond
and I raced home faster than all my sisters. We were
the first to see Father and Little Quang at the picture
window, and beside them . . .

Mother!

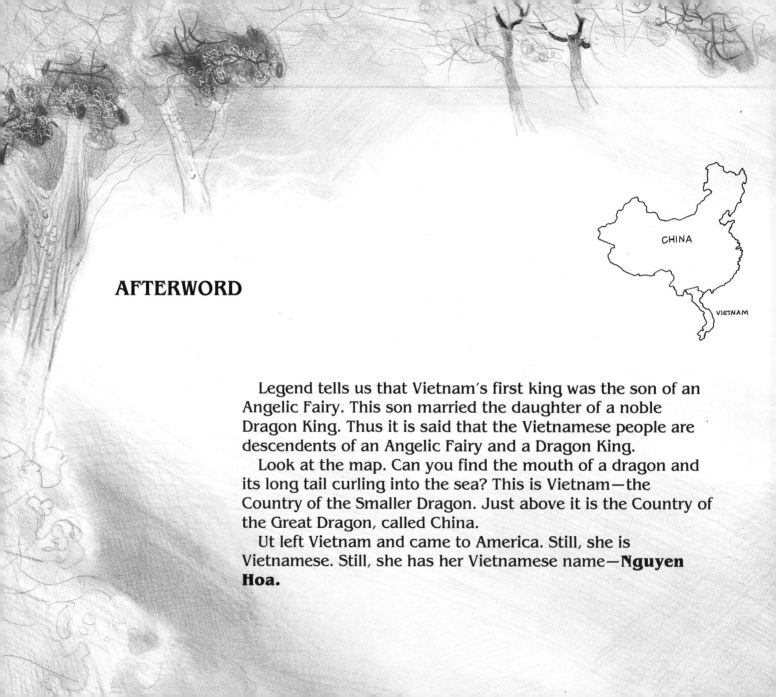

AFTERWORD

Legend tells us that Vietnam's first king was the son of an Angelic Fairy. This son married the daughter of a noble Dragon King. Thus it is said that the Vietnamese people are descendents of an Angelic Fairy and a Dragon King.

Look at the map. Can you find the mouth of a dragon and its long tail curling into the sea? This is Vietnam—the Country of the Smaller Dragon. Just above it is the Country of the Great Dragon, called China.

Ut left Vietnam and came to America. Still, she is Vietnamese. Still, she has her Vietnamese name—**Nguyen Hoa.**

CHINA

VIETNAM

Nguyen is Ut's family name, chosen in honor of the last Vietnamese dynasty. Family is very important to the Vietnamese. Like the Nguyens, they put their family name first.

After Ut's family name comes her true name, **Hoa.** This is her very own name, meaning "flower." Hopefully, she will grow lovely and graceful as a flower, for her true name is a blessing and a wish.

But why does Hoa say "I am Ut"? **Ut** is the loving name for the smallest daughter or son—a name spoken at home. And what is the at-home name for eldest daughter? **Chi Hai.**

Every day, these names remind Ut of her homeland. And every autumn, the fiery leaves remind her of the *hoa-phuong* that grew near her Vietnamese home.

A graduate of Bread Loaf School of English in Vermont, *Michele Maria Surat* is a freelance writer and a high school teacher living in Richmond, Virginia. When a Vietnamese child with a tear-streaked face shared a photograph of her mother with "Miss Teacher," Ut's story began.

Compelled to relate the tale of these beautiful and courageous children, the author hoped to create a story that would promote understanding between Vietnamese children and their American peers, emphasizing an appreciation of the sensitive, determined spirits of the newcomers. This is the author's first book for children. Ms. Surat's dedication is "to the real Ut and all her sisters. With love."

Vo-Dinh Mai was born in Hue, Vietnam. As a boy he often visited a local woodcut artist, noting especially "the visible joy he exuded while working." Later, he studied at both the Ecole Nationale des Beaux-Arts and the Sorbonne in Paris. His paintings have been widely exhibited to international acclaim. Vo-Dinh Mai's books include the Christopher Award-winning *First Snow,* written by his wife Helen Coutant. Published as a writer, translator and illustrator, he now lives with his family at the foot of a mountain near Burkittsville, Maryland.